The Girl on the Dump

Tyree Campbell

The Girl on the Dump
by Tyree Campbell

All rights reserved. No part of this book may be reproduced or transmitted in any form or by any means, electronic or mechanical, including photocopying or recording or by any information storage and retrieval systems, without expressed written consent of the author and/or artists.

The Girl on the Dump is a work of fiction. Names, characters, places, and incidents are products of the author's imagination. Any resemblance to actual events or persons, living or dead, is entirely coincidental.

Story copyright owned by Tyree Campbell
Cover illustration "The Dump" by Teresa Jay
Cover design by Laura Givens

First Printing: January 2018
Second Printing: November 2024

Hiraeth Publishing
P.O. Box 1248
Tularosa, NM 88352
e-mail: hiraethsubs@yahoo.com

Visit www.hiraethsffh.com for online science fiction, fantasy, horror, scifaiku, and more. Stop by our online Shop for novels, magazines, anthologies, and collections. **Support the small, independent press...and your First Amendment rights.**

Also by Tyree Campbell

Nyx Series (Novels):
Nyx: Malache
Nyx: Mystere
Nyx: The Protectors
Nyx: Pangaea
Nyx: The Redoubt

Yoelin Thibbony Rescues (Novels)
The Butterfly and the Sea Dragon *
The Moth and the Flame *
*The Thursday Child**
Avatar
The End of Innocence

Lark Series (Novels)
The Desert Lark
The Iphajean Lark
The Justice Lark
The Traffic Lark
The Illusion Lark

Armed Do-gooder Series (Novels)
Bailey Belvedere
Sienne Vhartan (in late 2024)

Novels:
The Adventures of Colo Collins & Tama Toledo in Space and Time
The Adventures of Colo Collins & Tama Toledo in Love and in Trouble
Aoife's Kiss
The Breathless Stars
The Dice of God
The Dog at the Foot of the Bed
The Dog at War

Gallium Girl
Heir Apparent
Indigo
Iuliae: Past Tense
The Quinx Effect
Starwinders: Nohana's Heart
Starwinders: Nohana's Triangles
Thuvia, Maid of Earth
A Wolf to Guard the Door
The Woman from the Institute

Superheroine Novellas:
Bombay Sapphire 1 **
Bombay Sapphire 2 **
Bombay Sapphire 3 **
Bombay Sapphire 4 **
Bombay Sapphire 5
Oliva Sudden 1
Peridot 1
Peridot 2
Peridot 3
Peridot 4
Voyeuse 1
Voyeuse 2
Voyeuse 3

Collections:
AbracaDrabble
Drink Before the War
A Nice Girl Like You
(published by Khimairal, Inc)
Quantum Women *

Novellas:
*Becoming Jade
Cloudburst
Future Tense
The Girl on the Dump
The Martian Women
Sabit the Sumerian
Sarrow*

Poetry Collections
A Danger to Self and Others

SF for Younger Readers
*Pyra and the Tektites 1
Pyra (graphic novel) 1
Pyra and the Tektites 2
Pyra (graphic novel) 2
Pyra and the Tektites 3
Pyra and the Tektites 4
Pyra and the Tektites 5
Pyra and the Tektites 6*

* published by Nomadic Delirium Press

** published by Pro Se Press

All titles are available from the Shop at
www.hiraethsffh.com

For my brother Dandon
  after all these years . . .

The Girl on the Dump
Tyree Campbell

The girl lay sprawled atop the pile of refuse and dung just beyond the limits of the travelers' waystop as if she had been the last item cast there from the waste wagon. Tresh, on his way to the walled city of Nadua to seek employment as a tutor, paused in surprise at the side of the road when he spotted her there. Too much he had witnessed in his four decades, yet nothing quite like this.

Her garments consisted of a cheap white camisole and a man's undergarment, the leggings torn off at mid-thigh. She was unshod. Her hair, the color of wet straw, had been hacked short with a dull blade. A scrap of blue over her left ear might have been hers or a fragment of ribbon from the refuse heap. Her eyes were closed; he wondered whether they were pale, like his own. Certainly her skin was pale, although in the late morning sun it was beginning to redden. Bites from the hordes of flies that darted about over the refuse heap tormented her exposed skin. Only the gentle tremble of her breasts under the camisole, no larger than nectarines, indicated that she was still alive.

The mere sight of the girl stirred his loins with a memory. For just a moment he basked in the warmth of possibilities; then the reality of guilt cooled him. If he wished to slake his desires, taverns in nearby Nadua could provide the proper utensils, worn and tarnished though they might be. But she aroused within him another, more powerful need, one also derived from guilt but not so readily satisfied, and until now all but lost to him.

First, however, he had to be as certain as possible of the portents. From a skin dangling from his belt he took a tube of glass about the size of a finger, sealed with a cork. It was filled with clear water and some bits of colored wax, prepared just before he had begun his present journey. Briefly he examined them, and was forced to conclude that the girl bode neither good nor ill. She was something outside the realm of the reading he had taken.

Tresh stepped carefully, avoiding the refuse and holding his breath against the fetid air, and drew up beside her. Sleeping, was she, or drugged? He saw no sign of injury, although her positioning suggested that she had been slung unceremoniously to this spot, perhaps after having been rendered unconscious. He moistened the tip of his kerchief with cool water from a skin dangling from a strap across his shoulder, and touched it to a smudge on her cheek. Her eyelids fluttered, and lifted.

Unprepared for the sheer raw blue of her eyes, Tresh stumbled backwards.

He had never seen a cut and polished sapphire, but rather imagined one might be the color he saw in her eyes. He had heard that the most precious of such gems held depths that one might gaze into for hours, lost in daydreams and imaginings. Her eyes were like that. They overwhelmed the snub nose and the carnation slash of a mouth, the lips already chapped and cracked by the heat. Her sandy brown eyebrows were thick, almost masculine. Dabs of pale powder on her cheekbones seemed to serve no purpose—but Tresh did not trouble himself over any of these features. He was drawn back to her eyes.

The eyes took him in, and Tresh cringed

inwardly, embarrassed by his traveled appearance. He was wearing an outfit for a journey—long-sleeved gray pullover, black work trousers, and sturdy black hiking boots. The fabric was faded and worn in spots, the leather cracked around the ankles despite regular applications of saddle soap. He had not shaved since he began the journey three days ago. Gray streaked his sepia hair and splotched his stubble beard. In addition to the foodskin dangling from a leather strap, he carried at his left side a rumpled travel bag containing several articles of clothing and his few possessions. His heart ached. The girl was a young thing, and he was at that age when a man considers whether the company of such a one might rekindle some of his youth. It would not do to have her think him *too* old. But the ache soon passed, for he was coming to accept the other, better need he had of her, should she prove willing and competent.

"Are you hurt?" Tresh asked. The girl just looked at him, blinking in the bright sunlight, and he added, "Injured? Are you in pain?"

Her voice was coarsened by dryness. "I do not remember."

A blow to the head? Tresh wondered. More likely, a potion or spell to make her forget; but the portents would have indicated that. "My name is Tresh," he said, his tone inviting her to reciprocate.

She took the hand he offered. Her weight was insubstantial to the strength of his arm, yet her grasp was firm, and she was able to assist in the lifting to her feet. She was quite taller than he expected. To meet her eyes he had to look up slightly. Perhaps she was standing on something? But no, they were both on level ground.

Aware that he had held her hand too long for

simple assistance, he dropped it awkwardly and asked, just as awkwardly, "Do you remember your name?"

Twin sapphires flamed. "Of course I do!"

Tresh backed off a pace. "And it is?"

Her eyes softened. Presently they moistened. "I . . . do not . . ." Her expression said that she was avoiding the word "remember" because of her assertion of memory.

Tresh's smile flickered. "Sometimes I do not recall my own until well after midday."

She gave him a harsh look. "You should not drink so much."

Briefly she took in her surroundings. She did not, Tresh noted, inquire after her location or the means by which she had arrived at it. Instead she calmly took in the cobblestone road leading to and from the waystop, the refuse heap, the savannah that spread west toward the horizon, the encircling forest to the east with its leaves bright now in the gleaming sunlight. Here and there in the distance, barely discernable, clusters of farm folk labored with mattocks, while individuals carried buckets of water to the fields from the river that flowed past the walled city. Purple clouds in the western sky shadowed the land. A look of wonder came over her face, as if she had known about these sights, but was viewing them for the first time.

"Atonya," she said softly. "That is my name." Her wrinkled brow added, "I think."

The name struck Tresh like a hammerblow. It could not be true, of course—the portents would surely have cautioned him about her—but the girl, despite her apparent doubts, seemed to believe it. Though the sun warmed him, Tresh shivered. Furtively he scanned their surroundings. Only a few people were about on the cobblestone road, mostly travelers with business in one town or another, and no one wearing the official green and gold livery of Nadua. Anyone who espied him and the girl would suppose them to be father and daughter, despite her scant ragged apparel. He took her hand, and tightened his grip when she tried to withdraw.

"Come with me. We have to leave here."

She walked stiff-legged, resisting. "Who are you? Where are you taking me?"

But Tresh noted that she did not cry out for help. Because she did not credit what was happening to her? Or because she felt competent to deal with any threat he might present?

He did not answer her, nor did she repeat her questions or make any other protest. Ten minutes later, when they reached the point where the road intersected a rutted cart path leading toward the river, Tresh loosened his hold on her hand, and she pulled free. For a while she stood still, appraising him while she rubbed her wrist. Finally she gave herself a little nod.

"Where are we going?" she inquired.

The form of the question signifying that she had accepted his company, at least for the moment, Tresh addressed other needs. From his travel bag he withdrew a long brown cloak that he employed against chill winds, and pressed her to it. "I want to get us past the forest," he said, while she drew the cloak around her. "There's an inn not far beyond, where we can let rooms and I can take a fresh reading. We should be safe there."

He turned to go, and she fell in beside him. "Safe from what?"

"I'm not quite sure . . ."

"Atonya," she supplied, filling in the space he

gave her.

"Forgive me, but I do not think that can be your name."

She fell silent, for which Tresh was grateful. He had no answers for her, only the faintest glimmer of a suspicion. The danger to her was less physical than social. As impossible as it was for him to credit, she had been thrown away. As a discarded item she was subject to scavenging, and there were those who frequented refuse heaps who would find a use or a market for her. He doubted she was aware of this. But he was aware of her.

She needed more suitable clothing. The inn would have a bin of items left behind; they might find something suitable there, though she was of a size that reduced those odds considerably. Male attire, he decided, if she could be persuaded to wear it. His hand sought the comfort of the coin purse in a secure pouch in his trousers. With the girl now his voluntary responsibility, he had perhaps enough money for a month. He would have to find work, and soon, for he had neither the experience for nor the inclination toward brigandage or grifting.

The road led toward an ancient mixed forest. For an hour they walked it, their silence broken only by an occasional pensive murmur. Their feet—hers bare and his boot-clad—slipped now and then on the cobbles rounded by journeys. With the wind clutching them gently from the east, he caught the sharp scents of pine and fir, of banks of flowering shrubs in full bloom. These blended well with the scents of growing barley and wheat and clover. Spring had come, and now, this close to summer, was in full force. Tresh thought that appropriate to his condition, for he had needed something, someone, to give him a sense of rebirth. The girl beside him might retard the turning of the leaves in his years, might indeed signal a second budding.

In the forest, clumps of shadows reached them, split by beams of light. The cool air here afforded them some respite from the heat. Soon they came upon a travelers' bench under a pair of young oaks and Tresh, after a glance behind them to see whether they were being followed, broke the uneasy silence by inviting the girl to rest. They had not much farther to go to reach the inn and lodging, but he had already seen her stumble several times, probably from exhaustion. He sat down beside her, a prudent arm's length away. After a moment he took a small round loaf of black bread from the foodskin, tore it in half, and passed one piece to her. She took it and stared at it for several seconds.

"I'm sorry, but I'm fresh out of butter and cheese," said Tresh.

A smile tickled the corners of the girl's mouth. Her eyes thanked him as her teeth ripped free a chunk of bread. She devoured her half before Tresh had begun his. After a brief hesitation, he held his out to her. She looked at it, and licked her lips, and looked into his eyes, young sapphire into his lustreless gray.

"You must eat as well," she said.

Her voice now possessed a quality that drew him back to other years and locales, when his services were in demand among those who walked the halls of royal administration. There was strength and civility and empathy in her tone, one she might have taken with a favored servant who needed her understanding and compassion. Shaken, Tresh sat back, and gazed at her speculatively. Who, indeed, might she be? A mad notion regarding her true identity was beginning to coalesce in his mind, and he shook his head to dispel it, as one might brush crumbs from a shirt. Part of him hoped he was wrong; the other part was afraid he wasn't.

He took a bite from his bread and stuffed the remains back into the travel bag. A skin of wine came next, and she took a medium pull from it, making a face as she returned the skin. It was raw red table wine, without appellation, almost without nose; clearly her palate was accustomed to better. Tresh took enough to moisten his mouth and tease his thirst.

A brief silence followed, broken by the girl. Tresh saw her about to speak, and hoped she had recalled something from her memory, but she said, merely, "We should go."

Tresh gestured toward the west. The dark clouds there had gathered strength and size, and would verge upon the plains in two hours, probably less. At this time of year storms rushed and spent themselves quickly. Tresh's fingers curled around the amulet in his pocket. He had no protection from lightning for the girl. If the storm grew too quickly it might catch them before they reached the inn. Tresh stood, and pulled her up, and they returned to the road through the forest.

In silence they trod once more. The road soon gave onto a rolling grassland not yet claimed by cultivation. To the north, where a bank of trees fed from a creek, a small herd of abeks grazed, two of the horned males standing guard against predators. To the east and south the forest thinned to merge with the grassland, and the road was a reddish-brown ribbon looping for the inn that was just visible ahead through its windbreak of surrounding conifers. Tresh cast a glance backward. The storm was billowing now, but still over an hour away.

They had time.
 The thought struck him: time for what?
 Uncertainty prodded him like a broken promise. He had been traveling to Nadua without clear purpose, only a vague hope that the blemish on his reputation had not reached this far south, that he might gain a position as a tutor to one of the lower royals. Nadua offered a chance to start fresh. Now he had set aside that opportunity in favor of rescuing a derelict. Acting on impulse had brought him grief before. Yet what else could he have done?
 The girl beside him seemed to sense his fresh ambivalence. An anxious look crossed her features. She did not have to ask him whether something was wrong.
 Tresh erased all expression from his face, and told her nothing. He knew he ought to take a fresh reading, in wax or, better yet, lead, and he meant to do so after they gained the inn. Meanwhile, it was best for the portents that he limit his activities to walking.

༄ ༄ ༄

They reached *The Pine and Clove* not long after midday, with the storm surging in pursuit but half an hour away. The structure was sturdy if simple, the ceiling supported by thick, rough-hewn beams. supported in turn by thick, rough columns. It had been built around a garden with a pond, the doors to the stayrooms opening to the garden side for security, rather like a caravanserai. Most of the open bay that occupied the front side of *The Pine and Clove* was given over to a tavern, with a registration counter along the wall left of the main door. Candles in bronze sconces spaced regularly on the walls and paraffin lamps on the tables augmented the sunlight that poured in through the glazed clerestory windows. At the far end of the open bay, a barrier of movable screens isolated the pantry and the buttery. Within the bay, only a few patrons were sampling the brew and menu. A troupe of buskers had gathered at one table and was preparing to perform, their instruments and accessories strewn about. Tresh was somewhat relieved to note that no one paid him or the girl any attention. He ushered her to a bench by the front window and bade her sit down.

"Wait here," he instructed. "I'll see to our rooms."

"Wait," she said. A gamin smile creased her face, and quickly vanished. "Rooms?"

The question slapped at Tresh, its implications obvious. Yet he had seen nothing in the girl to suggest that an interlude was in the offing. He fought off the darkness of his past—the girl was neither ingenuous nor unaware. Where obscurity and disrepute had been his punishment, she might become his expiation, if he could but hold to his purpose.

"You have little gold and silver," she added hastily, before he could respond. Her voice had acquired something of a martial timbre, as if she were accustomed to command. "You must husband your resources." Then she averted her eyes, and blushed a little, and Tresh wondered whether the command or the color was more revealing of her.

"There may only be one bed," he contended.

"Then we shall deal with that circumstance as needs be," she countered. "Besides," and here she drew the cloak tighter, "you have seen much of me. Modesty is already compromised."

"Atonya, . . ."

"Yes," she said. "That *is* my name. Please: go

arrange for us a room. Please, Tresh."

The use of his name swept aside his misgivings. He turned and approached the counter, where a young man, likely the son of the inn's proprietor, was adding a small column of figures in a hidebound book. Tresh cleared his throat and, having gained attention, broached his needs.

"Not for a fortnight," said the young man, who acknowledged himself as Larro. "A hunting party arrives tomorrow. You may be required to free the room up then." His dark eyes flicked past Tresh's shoulder toward Atonya, though his face betrayed no expression. "One bed or two? We have both such stayrooms open." Seeing Tresh fumble for his coin purse, he added, "The let is the same."

Tresh hesitated, and realized the hesitation revealed too much. The young man already suspected him of unmeritorious intentions. To attempt to disabuse him of his suspicions would only serve to confirm them, so Tresh answered simply, "Two beds, please," and laid two broad silvers on the counter top.

In return Larro passed him a thick iron key, a knowing smile in his eyes only. Tresh scooped it up, and turned back to Atonya . . . who was gone.

Panic quickened Tresh. He scanned about, and soon found her associating with the buskers. A pile of clothing had been dumped on the table—costumes, by their look—and Atonya was poking through them. Already she had discarded her cloak in favor of an orange-and-brown wrap skirt that exposed one leg to the knee, and Tresh reckoned she had shucked herself out of the undergarment. She had also found an orange vest, and a sepia ribbon for her hair. He had no idea what else she might be looking for.

As Tresh moved toward her to intervene, one of the buskers acquired a flute and began to play, a flirtatious piece up and down scales interrupted with flighty passages. Someone else picked up a pair of hand drums, another a tambourine. Driven by rhythm, Atonya began an impromptu dance. Twirling, her wrap revealing first one leg and then the other, she wound her way among the tables, her bare feet scarcely imprinting the sawdust and dried herbs on the plank floor. She had swung a diaphanous scarf around her neck and shoulders, and removed her camisole. Bare skin under the vest flashed as she bent and swayed.

The few patrons began to give her their undivided attention. Her graceful, sinuous movements held them in thrall, snared by the vision of her. Even Tresh, whose powers should have made him immune to such wiles, found it difficult to take his eyes off her. She swayed toward him with little delicate movements of her hips that suggested a sensuality beyond her years, and he saw that her eyes were now enormous, the pupils dilated as if with drops of belladonna, the upper and lower lashes glistening with a kohl so black it reflected as silver in the candlelight from the sconces. He thought she recognized him, but the dilation seemed to distort her vision, so that she could not make of him a specific target for the invitation inherent in her movements.

Atonya was not blinking. A *frisson* shook Tresh, and his mind reeled. As the girl held her audience captive, so too was she held by the music that emanated from the buskers' instruments. Flute, drums, jangles . . . and some stringed instrument that Tresh could not identify was lightly plucked by the nimble fingers of one of the young men. The melody gathered momentum now, the strings and drum building together. Atonya began to swing her head, shaggy yellow hair whipping around her. It fairly crackled with the energy she emitted.

Tresh felt his heart stutter. There was a darkness here, something his runes had failed to detect. For just a moment he felt a pang of jealousy, that the girl was displaying to her audience a part of her that she had not shown to him. He felt outside of her—and perhaps that exclusion kept him from being pulled into the orbit of her dance.

Atonya writhed, her body no longer inviting but demanding now. A blackness visible only to Tresh emanated from her, its tendrils extending to her audience. The network drew them toward her. Several began to twist and cavort, and even Tresh felt the tug from her. He stood fast, white the knuckles of one hand that clutched at a rough wooden support. The power that issued from her was overwhelming. How could he have missed the signs? She should have glowed in warning for him. Yet he had seen nothing and detected nothing other than a girl at the cusp of her majority.

The tendrils grew in intensity, as did Atonya's power, which threatened now to engulf not only the open bay but the entire inn, and might not stop there. Tresh had to act quickly. Lowering his defenses, he allowed himself to be drawn to Atonya, and to the buskers. His own body twitched under the pull of the black tendrils, but his will kept him under control as he was tugged forward. When he was near enough, he snatched the flute from the flautist's hands, and the music abruptly stopped.

Atonya collapsed onto the floor as one dead. Dripping with perspiration, Tresh folded himself onto a bench and sat with his head in his hands, dark moist circles forming on the dusty floor directly under his nose. The maneuver to remove the busker's instrument was simple to conceive, exhausting to carry out. His powers, both mundane and arcane, faded. He needed rest.

Presently there came an unexpected touch at his armpits. He lacked even the strength or the will to open his eyes, and the possibility that he was in danger failed to rouse him. Hands tugged at him and lifted, and he struggled to his feet. The soft fabric of the scarf fluttered against his face as he was led from the tavern outside and along the cobblestone walkway that took them around the garden. His legs moved in slow motion; he saw his feet appear from under his torso and then disappear again. Strands of hair drifted across his mouth and stuck to the dampness there and on his skin. He wanted to brush them away, but his arm merely flapped and then hung limp at his side. Whoever was supporting him—it had to be the girl, but how, *how?*—began to push him up a flight of three steps and down another as they crossed over the stream that fed the pond. He turned his head and found an ear a scant hand's-breadth away, the pale shell poking through a mass of badly-cut, sweat-darkened yellow hair. The girl, he realized, taking each step in turn. He drew strength from her, and then fear, careful to conceal the latter, though if she were of the darker powers she would surely be aware of the caution within him. He stepped, and stepped again, and they reached the far rooms of the inn.

"I'm all right," Tresh managed, and disengaged from her to lean against a wall.

Sympathy moistened Atonya's eyes and invested her face with the pale pink of a spring sunrise. "You should not dance so," she clucked, and shook her head. "At your age . . ."

Tresh's face warmed. He had hoped to avoid her regarding him as too old, because it lightened his heart to suppose that she might look at him fondly. He wondered whether she knew his secret thoughts, whether she could identify the cause of the color in his face.

"I'm not *that* old," he protested.

"No," the girl agreed easily. "You are not. But for the *mortiaria* you should be much younger. Only those who are ignorant of their own mortality should participate in it. Which room is ours?"

Tresh gasped. "*Mortiaria?*"

"That is what you were dancing, yes. Which room?"

Tresh looked for a number, found it. "That one." The girl plucked the key from him, inserted it into the keyhole, and turned it. The locking mechanism creaked, breaking free of rust. The door swung open of its own accord, and they fairly stumbled through the opening, Tresh again on the verge of collapse. Once inside the room, he spied a pair of narrow four-posters, the heads abutting the right wall, and lurched toward the nearest one, the girl following after she secured the door. Tresh pitched his travel bag onto the comforter that covered the bed and sprawled on his back across the foot of the bed, mumbling.

Atonya came to a halt, hovering over him, her expression a mix of concern and impatience. Her vest was slightly askew, and through the diaphanous crimson scarf slung carelessly about her shoulders Tresh caught glimpses of the inner swells of her breasts. "I can't understand you," she complained.

Tresh forced himself to avert his eyes. He had

strength enough for that, at least. Already the intimacy of their quarters was dwelling on him, lapping at his resolve. He knew—he had known since finding her—that there would come a choice between his own desires and his hunger for expiation. He could not countenance the pursuit of both. The original purpose of his journey all but forgotten now, he was compelled to continue what he had begun with the girl.

Over her arm Atonya carried the cloak he had given her. He nudged it with his hand. "Cover yourself," he instructed, his tone gruff.

The girl obeyed. "What were you saying just now?"

Tresh thought back. "An incantation," he answered vaguely. It was already having some effect on him; he felt his vitality returning.

A pale eyebrow arched. "You are an arcanist?"

The truth, thought Tresh. *Tell her the truth. See how she reacts.*

"I see the tapestry of existence," he said slowly. "And I am able to pluck the threads of it, hopefully favorably. Arcana provides my vision in these matters, and the more I understand of it, the better my vision."

Atonya stood with fists against hips, challenging him. "For example?"

Tresh cupped his hands together. Water filled the basin they formed. "Drink?" he offered.

She bent, and put her face to the water. Droplets spilled from her chin when she straightened. "Like spring water," she gasped.

Tresh took a few sips, then spread his hands. The remaining water vanished. His hands were dry.

"Can you teach me to do that?" the girl asked.

"Perhaps," said Tresh. He rose and moved to

the fireplace. A small broom hung from a bronze hook on the wall beside the chimney, and he used it to clear ashes from the hearth, exposing yellow fire bricks. From his travel bag he extracted a plain iron goblet with an indentation in the lip for pouring, and set it on the hearth. A tall, clear drinking glass joined it. Finally, he drew a misshapen chunk of lead from the travel bag, and squatted on his haunches in front of the yellow bricks.

"What—are you doing?" asked Atonya.

Tresh placed the lead chunk into the goblet. A brief incantation while pointing his finger caused the goblet to glow. The light from it lent a sheen to their faces. Inside the bowl, the lead collapsed and melted. At Tresh's command the glass began to fill with clear water. When it was full, he reached for the goblet, and Atonya screamed.

"Don't touch it!"

Startled, Tresh pulled his hand back, almost spilling the glass of water. "Death's Door, girl!" he swore, and recovered. "Only the metal within the cup is hot, not the goblet itself."

Carefully he allowed five droplets of molten lead to spill into the water. Each droplet congealed as it plunged hissing toward the bottom of the glass, and Tresh studied the irregular shapes as they formed. "I could have used paraffin," he told Atonya, "but lead gives a stronger reading."

Atonya dropped to one knee beside him. "And what does this tell you?" she asked.

Her body heat gloved his senses, disrupting his ability to read the portents. In a ragged voice he uttered a barrier spell, and gathered himself behind it. In the wash of the powers Tresh had invoked, the girl's aura began to appear, a cloud of burnt orange enveloping her, though she appeared not to notice it. The color, indicative of change, of the injection of chaos into order, altered Tresh's interpretation of the silvery shapes in the glass of water. He trembled, reading them. They spoke of perils to be overcome by himself and Atonya, but the consequences of confronting those perils remained hidden from him. He was unable to foresee whether he and the girl would succeed, whether either or both would die in the attempts. The shapes of the droplets also confirmed his suspicion that the girl had come from the House of Nadua, but they refused to reveal whether she was the princess and heir to the throne or merely one of the doubles.

Uncertain now, Tresh sat back and stared into the hearth. Atonya's glow had faded, but light flashed outside and momentarily cast her shadow over him. As thunder began to rock the inn, the girl clutched at Tresh, and crouched behind him. She cried out when another bolt flashed, and with her cry of fear the candles in the wall sconces took flame.

Tresh barely managed to conceal his astonishment. Atonya's ready immersion into the darker aspects of the *mortiaria* suggested a weakness that a simple spell might override, but the spontaneous ignition of candles spoke of a far more sinister shadow within her. At some point during her late adolescence, she probably had been in contact with a black mage.

A black mage who was someone within the royal entourage of the House of Nadua. The tutor to the heir to the throne? Such a one could go wherever he wished without hindrance. Just as long ago he, Tresh, had been able to spirit the Princess of Eridania into his quarters for their trysts. Tresh closed his eyes, locking within him the pain of his transgression. Erin of Eridania had been of age, and more than willing, and unencumbered by another relationship, as much was true. But she had been his charge. The fault was his, and his alone.

"Why do you weep?" asked Atonya, scratching at a tiny red welt on her forearm.

He gave her a glimpse at the truth. "You remind me of something I lost."

Her face screwed up. "Some*thing*? Not some*one*?"

Tresh fished in his travel bag and withdrew a small amulet dangling from thin straps of leather. With his finger he motioned for her to turn around, and she complied without protest, turning back to face him after he had tied the straps at the nape of her neck. Her hand went to the amulet, and held it up for inspection—a polished peridot set in silver. She looked a question at him.

"I should have given you that sooner," said Tresh apologetically. "In a few minutes those bites will trouble you no more."

She met his gaze. "Thank you."

Tresh got back to his feet, and pulled her up. Outside the storm continued unabated. Rain lashed the unshuttered window, and lightning dazzled the surrounding trees. Atonya stood close by him, not quite touching, and after a moment Tresh moved away, toward one of the sconces. Atonya had kindled the flame in this one and in the others, but whether the power within her derived from light or dark, he could not now say for certain. The girl's fear of the storm was natural and understandable, and that fear, combined with an innate if raw ability to wield the powers of arcana, might have set the candles aflame. But that sort of untrained control over the elementals also stemmed from blacker aspects. Who was she, then?

A clap of thunder buffeted the inn. The glazing in the window rattled as raindrops drummed against it, powered by gusts of wind that bent the windbreak pines. Atonya, braver now, turned her back to the storm and drifted to the farther of the two beds from the entrance, and sat down, plucking delicately at the wrap skirt to adjust it over her legs.

Her voice came low but firm, the voice of one who had the authority to expect a fair answer. "Tell me what you learned from your metal," she said.

Tresh became a peripatetic thinker. Around the room he wandered, at no time drawing too close to her while he spoke.

"There are several questions to be answered," he said at last, while lightning illuminated his face from time to time. "First, your name. I accept that your name is Atonya."

"Thank you," she said primly, interrupting.

"Please. There is more to the name than the name. Please forgive me the form of this next question, but: do you know who you are?"

Eyelashes still clotted with kohl fluttered. "I . . . I live in . . . there are a lot of rooms. One of them is mine." She glanced around her, and added, somewhat distastefully, "It is better than this one."

"I am certain of that," said Tresh. "Now close your eyes. Look at your room. Can you see it now?" Atonya gave a little nod, and he continued, "Tell me what you see."

For several seconds she did not answer. A note of incredulity crept into her tone when finally she spoke. "It is . . . well-appointed, there is a great bed, larger than these two together, with broad and thick pillows filled with down. Sheets, a cover, a veil . . . no, four veils, hanging between the posts. An armoire of fine dark wood. There is . . . there are curtains of the same color as the bedcover, they hang across a great window that looks out over a courtyard . . . no, over . . . over a city." She opened her eyes abruptly. "What is this place, Tresh? Why should I see this place?" When he did not respond, she cried, "Oh, tell me! Please!"

Tresh paused beside the window. The calm of the storm now appeared centered over the inn, while wind gusts bent the surrounding pines like bows, and rain sieved through the needles. He cast a look back at the girl, who anxiously awaited his response.

"What color are the curtains?" he asked.

Her jaw dropped. ". . . what? They're . . . they're blue. They're blue, just like my eyes, so my father says . . ." Her voice trailed off to a whisper. "My father. The king . . . the king of . . . of . . ."

"Nadua?" Tresh said gently.

Atonya nodded. "The King of Nadua." Her face twisted in anguish. "But why would he throw me away? How *could* he . . .? *Why?*"

"I don't think he did," said Tresh.

More questions twisted Atonya's face into a dark mask of confusion and anger, and darkened her eyes almost to indigo. While she struggled for words, Tresh sat down beside her on the bed. Hands clasped between his knees, he hunched forward and gazed down at the dried herbs sprinkled over the raw wood floor. "You have a double," he told her. "Someone to take your place credibly at various public functions. Probably over the course of your life you've had several, as you yourself in growing changed in shape and appearance. Every so often, a new double was installed to reflect those changes, and the predecessor was discarded. And now I suspect the current double has been established in your stead, and this time it's you who were discarded as the double—"

"Oh, that's horrible!"

"But not an uncommon practice."

She twisted on the bed to face him. "But . . . what happened to the others?"

Her altruism secretly pleased him. "Maybe they were sold," he told her, without conviction. "Maybe they were cast onto the refuse heaps. I doubt anyone knows, now."

"My father . . . ?"

Tresh shook his head. "Someone on his staff would see to their disposal. It's very probable that your father knows nothing about the details."

"Someone on staff," mused Atonya. "Like the vizier?" And immediately she added, aloud and to herself, "Why did I say that?"

"It could well be the—"

Atonya shot to her feet, startling Tresh. "I remember!" she cried, and the flames in the candles momentarily brightened. A bolt of lightning struck one of the pines, investing her face and skin with a spectral white glow. A crack of thunder pierced the room, resounding within the walls like a trapped animal. Atonya pressed her hands to her head, whispering, "Oh, I remember."

Tresh muttered a charm to dampen the sound, and stood up. The air continued to crackle for several seconds after the echoes of the thunder had faded. Atonya's eyes regained focus, and gradually her composure returned. Glistening sapphires came to regard Tresh, now standing beside the nightstand between the two beds, and well away from her.

A frown crossed her brow. "Why are you over there?" she asked.

Outside, the wind picked up again. The storm was moving on.

Tresh said, "Tell me about the vizier."

"There is not much to tell," said Atonya. "His name is Verlang. He has been a friend of my father for many years, more than I have been alive. When I was six, I was placed in his charge for education and protection."

She sat back down on her bed, and made a little peremptory gesture to Tresh to seat himself, which he did, on his bed this time. "I am the presumptive heir to Nadua," she went on. "A male heir would take precedence over me, but as it happens, I have but a sister, Risse, who is ten, and there will be no more, for my mother is unable now. And I . . . knew about the doubles," she added, her voice trembling now, but whether in sorrow or in anger, Tresh could not say. "It just . . . never occurred to me that they would be sold, or thrown away, or . . . Tresh, would Verlang have killed them?"

"He might have had them killed," Tresh conceded. "But it's more likely that he incanted a spell or gave them a potion to wipe their minds, and sold them, or . . . as was done with you."

"But he did not wipe my mind," Atonya pointed out.

Tresh looked away. "I imagine he thought he did, but . . . the spell or potion did not take."

Atonya shook her head. "No," she said, and now there was a touch of iron in her tone. Eyes now dark blue bored into his. "You are being evasive. You have been evasive. This is not the first question I have put to you that you have answered weakly or not at all."

Tresh felt a tendril of darkness extend in his direction. Once again a faint orange glow enveloped Atonya. She herself seemed oblivious to the changes. *She does not know,* he thought, astonished. Incongruously, the room brightened, and for a moment he wondered whether she had sparked the candle flames. But the storm was abating. The rain had stopped, the windbreak pines swayed in the remnants of the wind, and sky was lightening.

"I am aware of that failing," said Tresh. He got up and eased by her, and began to drift around the room, taking stock of their surroundings. Alongside the door jamb hung a pull cord for summoning a chamber maid. The only furniture other than the beds was the nightstand against the wall between the two beds, and an old wooden chair that had been abandoned to a corner. Tresh doubted whether the chair would support Atonya, and certainly not himself. Wooden pegs in the side wall opposite the beds invited them to hang up their clothing. He peered into a curtained alcove next to the window, where the outer wall was corbelled so that the alcove overhung. Within he found a fresh chamber pot and a large wooden tub for bathing. A pair of sloping gutters led outside. Openings in the rafters allowed unpleasantness to filter out through the eaves.

Seeing the tub reminded Tresh that he had not bathed since beginning his journey. The girl's glare reminded him that he had not suitably responded to her charge. A grumble from his stomach threatened to override both concerns.

Rather to his astonishment, Atonya laughed. The tendril he had sensed from her a moment ago now withdrew, and her aura faded out. Tresh cocked a thick black eyebrow at her.

"Can you not conjure a meal?" she asked, with gentle irony.

For a moment Tresh glowered at her in mock annoyance. Then he flashed a smile. "No more than I can conjure bath water," he told her. "I am able to survive through various hardships, so long as I do not overtax myself. No more than that. To turn the tapestry of existence to my own profit and pleasure requires a submission to . . ."

"Yes?" Atonya took a step forward, her expression at once eager and insistent. "Yes? Tell me! Put an end to your evasions, arcanist!"

Tresh fixed his pale eyes on hers. Despite her agitation, neither tendrils nor aura had appeared. Atonya genuinely desired answers to her questions. But if he revealed to her the full potential of arcana, was she strong enough to resist the tugs from the seeds of darkness that Verlang must have implanted within her?

The sound of her voice lifted him from his fears for her. She was looking at him expectantly now, with just a trace of impatience in the tiny furrows above the bridge of her nose. The challenge she had presented him was at once frightening in its implications yet hopeful in its possibilities. It also raised within him a question he knew he should have identified earlier: why would Verlang replace Atonya with a double? While he considered this, he tried to satisfy the girl's sudden craving for knowledge.

"I can conjure items I do not actually need, Atonya," he said softly. "Clothing for you, for instance. A meal for us. I can do these things." His right arm flinched; he had almost reached out to touch her. "But they would be vanities, Atonya, weaknesses. Inevitably they would lead to more vanities, and to luxuries. To riches and power. And inevitably to a darkness that I cannot begin to describe to you. Arcana is a tool, not a means to an end." He smiled benignly. "And the means to the end of assuaging our hunger is to go downstairs and peruse the menu." He held out his arm to her. "Shall we?"

♋   ♋   ♋

Tresh and Atonya seated themselves at a corner table, away from the flurries of activity that included brief song and dance performances by the buskers. Already perhaps a dozen patrons had drifted into the tavern bay to drink ale and watch the impromptu show. A serving girl in a pale blue smock approached Tresh, and he rendered his order without a menu—a basket of bread rolls, butter, slices of meat and cheese, a pitcher of cool water. Atonya gave him a frown as the girl sauntered away.

"I was thinking of something more substantial," said Atonya.

Tresh shook his head. "We eat what they eat," he told her, and made a little gesture toward the other patrons. "We're just a couple of wayfarers, nothing more."

Atonya set her jaw. "Are you going to talk to me?" she said severely.

"Presently," said Tresh, fiddling with a butter knife.

She snatched the knife away and glared at him. A moment later, she shed the cloak he had given her; underneath it she was still attired in the clothing she had acquired from the buskers—the long orange and brown skirt, and the orange vest, which she did not bother to tighten around her.

Tresh forced himself to avert his eyes, and was

saved from possible heated discussion with Atonya by the serving girl, who arrived at their table. She placed the ordered items on the table before them, accepted a silver coin from Tresh, and departed. He poured water for each of them, and held out his hand for the knife. Not quite pouting, Atonya placed the knife on his palm, wooden handle towards him, and leaned back, arms folded across her chest, waiting.

"I thought you were hungry," said Tresh, buttering a roll.

"For answers."

Tresh nodded slowly. "Very well. I shall be blunt. You have a gift for the use of arcana. This gift may be innate, or it may have been infused into you. Either way, you have not yet learned to control it. I should like to instruct you in the means of control and application."

The girl leaned forward, arms crossed on the table top, as she peered into his eyes. "I detect a note of reservation in your voice." When he did not respond, she asked, "Infused by whom?"

"Verlang, possibly."

"And . . . why does that make you hesitate?"

"Atonya—"

She smiled. "Ah! I think I like the way you say my name." She took a slice of ham from the basket and gnawed a piece free, chewing slowly. "Tell me," she urged.

"I hesitate because your gift may have come from the dark side of arcana," said Tresh, and added quickly, as concern lined her face, "That does not ally you with the darkness, Atonya, believe me. It is but a seed that Verlang has planted. It may be cultivated in either direction, but because it was he who planted it, you may show a tendency toward . .

. well . . ."

"You are frightening me."

"Fear can engender a healthy respect for . . . what's the matter?"

Her eyes had widened and darkened. She shifted to one side, as if to hide behind him. Her whisper was barely audible. "A man just entered," she told him. "He is at the registration counter. I have seen him before."

Tresh slowly turned until he could study the newcomer without appearing to do so. His doeskin trousers fit him without a wrinkle, and rich embroidery in gold thread adorned his long-sleeved green tunic. Spurs of silver clutched at the heels of his brown leather boots: he had ridden here. Tresh estimated his age as midway between Atonya's and his own. His golden hair was trimmed so that it hung evenly all around, and just touched his collar. He bore no weapons, but perhaps he did not require them; the way he carried himself all but announced with fanfare that he represented and was supported by high authority. The colors of his tunic said that the authority was the royal house of Nadua.

"He is . . . he is . . . ," tried Atonya, and whimpered in frustration. "Oh, I can't remember!"

Tresh, fearful that her uncontrolled emotions might spark another lighting of candles, or worse, reached across the table and took her hands in his. They were soft and cool, but warming because her blood now flowed more quickly. She blinked just once, and her eyes lightened back to sapphire.

Tresh found himself unable to speak; she was doing something to him. But what?

A memory came to him, unbidden, of Erin of Eridania in her boudoir. It filtered through the wall of suppression he had built over the years, and heat suffused his face. He knew it gave him away, yet still he could not speak, could not mutter the brief incantation that would lock that memory back in its place.

She frowned, though her eyes did not darken, nor did she release his hands. "Oh," she said. "I see."

Tresh jerked his hands back, and almost spilled the pitcher of water.

"Be careful," hissed Atonya. "I don't want him to notice me." Her face twisted in distress. "I just wish I could think why."

Tresh's voice shook. "I want to know what you saw," he said.

"Later, perhaps. Let us address ourselves to the food, such as it is."

He frowned at her. "This is perfectly good fare."

Again she looked distressed. "Oh, yes, of course it is. I didn't mean . . . I'm sorry. And thank you for seeing to my needs." She punctuated this by cutting open a roll, stuffing it with meat and cheese, and taking a bite.

They ate in a silence Tresh had no wish to break. The girl had caught a glimpse of his past, but did she understand how it now affected him and his outlook and his present motives? He had made his choice; he would not repeat his transgression. Instead, Atonya was to be his atonement. Even her name was fitting.

Still, desire gnawed at him. He had rationalized his encounters with Erin of Eridania on the basis that their affection had grown toward one another to the point where an intimate interlude was the next step, even if that step were ethically awry. A dark part of him sought another rationalization, even now, with regard to Atonya. Where had it come from? He had fought this battle, and had won. Why was it cropping up again?

Atonya, he concluded: the darkness within her was projecting itself into his vulnerability, seeking a crack or a flaw to exploit. But to what end? Did it wish to prevent him from tutoring her? Or did it mean to drive him toward her, succumbing to himself, and thereby drive her further into a darkness from which it would be even more difficult to escape? Tresh longed to take another reading at this moment, but he had left his tools in the room.

Fighting back by force of will, Tresh clenched his teeth and gave a tight but violent shake of his head. No, he would do it right this time. Given the chance, he would tutor Atonya and then leave.

Do you hear me, Darkness?

"Do I dare inquire into your thoughts?" said Atonya, as she finished her roll.

Tresh blinked. The man who had been standing at the registration counter was no longer there. Had he taken a room? Tresh gave the bay a quick glance, without finding the man.

"Can you remember his name yet?" he asked Atonya.

A look of loathing came over her face. In the middle of chewing, she stopped, and for a moment Tresh thought she was about to disgorge. But she swallowed hard, and took a long draw from a mug of water. Her voice cracked when she spoke, a single word.

"Verlang."

The tone of her voice spooked Tresh even more than the name. He knew some spells, and he possessed some runes, but until he knew more about the assets of his adversary, he dared not invoke anything and risk alerting Verlang to his presence.

"What is he doing here?" whispered Atonya.

Tresh looked inward. "I do not sense that he is aware of us," he said at last. "A hunting party is due to arrive tomorrow, and perhaps he is here in advance of it."

"Then my father the"—here she paused and glanced around to see if anyone could overhear, and continued, her next word hushed, as she leaned closer—"king will be here. This does not bode well. You should check your portents again, arcanist."

The tavern door opened, this time admitting two men and a young woman. The men wore the livery of Nadua. Aside from long, loose yellow hair, the woman might have been Atonya's twin. Or, thought Tresh, in a residue of uncertainty, Atonya herself.

"Do nothing to draw attention to yourself," he ordered, his voice low. "Keep your eyes down, your face down."

She picked up the bread knife, and held it as if she were prepared to use it if necessary. "Tell me what's wrong," she insisted.

"You just entered the tavern."

The news failed to alarm her. "What else?"

He frowned, puzzled. "What do you mean?"

"Something else bothers you."

Tresh shook his head.

"Look at me," she said, and he did. "I *am* Atonya."

Reluctantly he nodded. "But why would Verlang discard the real one and retain the imposter?" he asked, mostly to himself. "What does she have that you do not?"

Atonya patted her head. "Hair, I daresay."

"I told you not to look," he growled.

"They are headed into the tavern."

Tresh took a deep breath and muttered an incantation. By the time he had finished, his upper torso rocked slowly from side to side, and his eyes were on the verge of scrolling up.

"Tresh?" worried Atonya.

"Give me a moment," he gasped weakly.

She leaned in his direction, her arm steadying him.

"Don't," he whispered. "You'll call attention to us."

"And you're not?" She clutched his shoulder, holding him in place. "Close your eyes," she ordered, her tone brooking no argument. "Breathe. In, out. Slowly."

His shoulders slumped. He sat back. She was what he saw when he opened his eyes again, her short hacked hair now as black as obsidian. He risked a quick glance toward the entrance and saw that the two men and the False Atonya had taken a table near the ale kegs diagonally across the tavern from himself and Atonya. With several other tables intervening, he decided the chances of notice and discovery were reduced enough for them to return to normal behavior.

"What was that curse you uttered?" Atonya asked him.

Now he tried the bread and butter. "No curse," he replied. "I changed your hair color."

She tugged short tresses from around her ears. "So you did. May I look at them now?"

"Just don't be obvious about it," he cautioned. "Tell me what you notice about her."

A minute passed, and another. Finally Atonya said, "She is me. I don't know what you want from me. What is it that I should say?"

Belatedly Tresh grasped that she would not be aware of what he was seeing in the False Atonya,

because the comportment and carriage of royalty was common to both women as a matter of status and upbringing.
"The two men are probably her bodyguards," said Tresh. "Observe her expression. To her they are subservient, of lower status. See how silent she is, and how she pays no attention to her surroundings. She would not deign to include them in her thoughts. She is waiting."
"For Verlang."
"That is likely."
Atonya's brow furrowed. "You are saying that I did not notice these things because I, too, carry myself like that."
"I meant no offense."
"Am I truly that aloof?" she asked.
"That's not what I was—"
"Because I have never abused or distanced myself from a member of the household staff in my life," she snapped. "That is not my way. Yes, I have seen others. I have seen my father and mother on occasion. But I myself grew up with some of the children, I played with them."
She fell silent, eyes cast down at the table and the plate before her. Her breathing came shallow.
"Atonya?" Tresh fretted.
"Memories," she said softly, and sighed. "Memories. Sometimes they are a trickle, sometimes a flood. I wonder who I am, Tresh."
The sound of his name from her lips quieted him. Two or three times she had addressed him, but not in the tone of uncertainty, as if she were gently nudging him for answers to questions she was as yet unable to voice. Within him, pity blended with compassion; he wanted to reach out and touch her, to reassure her. It pained him to

realize that he would not do that.

But there was something else that he still could not quite identify—a point of reasoning the logic of which for the moment was cloudy. It had to do with why Verlang had promoted the substitute.

Her hand on his startled him. He looked down at it, and she withdrew.

"You are troubled," she said.

His nod admitted as much. "There is an exit on the other side of the buttery," he said. "It leads to the rooms. I want us to leave before Verlang returns."

Without hesitation Atonya got to her feet, donned her cloak, and looked at him expectantly. Her unquestioning compliance pleased him. No explanations demanded, no worries. He gestured her toward the buttery and walked behind her, to screen her from view.

♋   ♋   ♋

Foreboding accompanied Tresh on the way back to their room. He tried to shunt his mind from it, fearing that Verlang would detect his presence. They splashed through puddles—raindrops continued to drip from the roof of the inn—and he felt a chill. He wondered whether it came from the storm that had passed recently, or from a feeler cast around by Verlang. Try as he might, Tresh could not banish the vizier's name from his mind. Almost certainly Verlang was now aware that someone of the power of arcana was nearby. As soon as he settled on a direction, he might well seek them out.

They reached the room. Again Atonya took the key from him and opened the door. Quickly Tresh pushed her inside, then followed, shutting the door firmly behind them. She took two more steps into the room and whirled around, a protest already on her lips.

Tresh pressed a finger against his own lips, a signal for silence. A gesture from him bade her sit on her bed. He went to the window and cautiously looked outside. Nearby pines bent a little under the weight of the water on their needles. Above them, dusk was settling over the land. Several people walked about on a cobblestone path that wound through the small flower gardens. None of them were Verlang. Tresh turned back around, and leaned against the wall, out of sight. A nod from him told Atonya that it was all right to speak.

She had only a question for him. "What now?"

Long seconds passed while he considered his response. There was much regarding her latent abilities that he might tell her, or refrain from telling her. In the matters of arcana she was raw, unskilled, and that, combined with knowledge he might impart to her, made her potentially a threat to her own survival, and perhaps to his. But she posed the same danger should he reveal nothing to her, for she would respond emotionally to circumstances, without control or training.

Before he found the words, Atonya rose from the bed and approached him. Within arm's reach of him she drew up, and placed a hand gently against his chest. Her sapphire eyes seemed to bore into his, and he wondered whether she was unwittingly casting a spell. His lips felt parched; he licked them.

"You are afraid for me," she said. "It is this darkness within me that you spoke of."

He could but nod, once.

"Train me," she told him, in the tone of an order. "Teach me."

She was standing too close to him; she was Erin

of Eridania, her affection for him a ghost of emotion. It sifted through him like a zephyr through a sieve. Erin of Eridania was lost to him, but this girl before him, this young woman—

"*No,*" Tresh half-shouted, and spun away from Atonya. He strode to his own bed and came to stand on the far side of it, safe from her approaches. His heart raced; he had almost succumbed—but to what? To her wishes, or his own desires? His purpose was to teach, to train. But not to have feelings, not to love. Not again, he reminded himself, and drew strength from the reminder.

Atonya turned around, arms limp at her sides. Her expression blended sadness with pain, the pain of rejection, even though she had made no offer. The expression confirmed to Tresh the wisdom of stepping away from her, of evading what she might have said. Or what he might have said.

He slipped a tendril free and sent it into her, seeking the source of her emotions. Gradually it became clear that the dark seed planted within her had not sparked her approach to him. Whatever she had projected, whatever he had sensed, had come from Atonya herself. Feeling rather worse now, he withdrew the tendril. Training her risked emotional entanglement. To restore himself, he would have to be strong. He would have to be cold.

"Sit down, please," he said. His voice sounded hollow to him; his throat felt constricted. The onset of tears? But his eyes remained dry. They watched her while she sat down on her own bed, watched dispassionately the gentle sway of her breasts under the vest, visible through the open cloak. He found himself able to look at her as one might regard a statue, a sculpture.

"I am sitting down," she hinted.

"That darkness within you is but a seed," he told her. "It has not sprouted as yet. It is not yet a part of you. But it will become so, and it cannot be removed, not even by the arcanist who planted it there. To cope, you must learn to control it, to use its powers for light rather than for darkness. I can train you to do this. But it will take time."

"How much time?" she wanted to know.

"Days. Months. It depends on the student, on you."

His mind shouted to him: *tell her!*

He rejected the command, and said only, "There is something I must do, Atonya. You cannot help me directly, but you can ease my task by controlling your emotions. Do not allow yourself to feel; do not concern yourself with me. Remain awake and alert."

Pale eyebrows bunched at the bridge of her nose. "What are you going to do?"

He found a smile to reassure her. "Something arcane. But during it I will not be able to help you. For that reason, it is important that you do not allow your emotions to take hold."

"Why?"

The question he had dreaded. He had no choice but to temporize. "It is best I explain after I have completed my task," he said.

She looked glum. "Promise?"

He nodded.

"Say it," she said, ordering and yet pleading.

Tresh sat down on the bed and opened his travel bag. From it he withdrew an amulet, a garnet the size of a walnut in a silver setting, on a silver chain. This he hung around his neck.

"Tresh?"

He forced himself to look at her. He feared his

answer might prove a lie. Still, he gave it to her.

"I promise, Atonya. Now, I must engage. At some point I may emit sounds, or even speak. Pay no attention to me."

Atonya laid back on her bed. Her sapphire eyes remained full of questions, and for a moment he feared she would ask at least some of them. Gradually, acceptance softened her face, for which he was grateful.

"I shall rest, then," she declared. "And wait for you."

His right hand enclosed the amulet. His lips moved with silent words. His eyelids drooped, and closed. Under them, black reigned. He was scarcely aware of his breathing. One thought prevailed: seek. Darkness stretched, and became a tendril, the way a living glob of protoplasm extends a pseudopod.

Darkness began to fade to the light of late dusk.

Two men, he sought, and a young woman—the False Atonya, he was certain of that now. They still sat at the table in the tavern. He saw them as if he were looking at them through a pipe, the image a clear circle blurred around the edges. Closer he drew, his senses through the tendril attuned to the trio. Sounds reached him—the chewing of food, the slurping and gulping of drinks—but only a few words, none of interest to him. He waited, and watched, and listened.

Presently the False Atonya got up and moved out of the circle. Tresh did not follow; instead, he remained focused on the two men. Already a *frisson* of wrongness was creeping up his spine, a spider of warning, perhaps of premonition—something he knew he should recognize. Unable at the moment to determine its source, he set it on the verge of his consciousness, to consider it later.

Now that the girl had left, the two men were talking.

"Ar Master claim she be ready," said the one with black hair and a single dark eyebrow that grew across his forehead. He spoke with an accent from a coastal duchy that Tresh recognized. "Oy be not so sure, Byuly. Not so sure."

The other man, shorter and stockier, merely shrugged. His own accent was coastal as well, but from further south. "We has ar orders, and half ar money. What care we be she ready or no?"

"He be paying oos the other half, then, d'ye reckon?"

For a few seconds, Byuly did not answer. Instead, he took a long gulf of ale, and swallowed slowly, his brow furrowed in thought. Finally he set the mug down. "Here be me thinking, Samyun, old dog. For this day's work, witnesses be a risk."

Samyun sat back as if he had been struck. "He be doing oos, then, d'ye reckon?"

Byuly did not respond. Instead he hunched his broad shoulders and glanced furtively around the room. He seemed to be sniffing the air. "Be ye feeling that?" he asked.

His companion frowned. "Oy be somat chill, zall."

"Be black feeling," said Byuly, still looking around. "Ar Master, mayhap." He shivered, and clasped both hands around his ale mug, his knuckles whitening.

"We be gone we does it, then, d'ye reckon? Far and fastly."

Byuly nodded, and stared down at his ale, his single eyebrow bunched like a small animal.

Tresh pulled back. The man named Byuly had sensed a presence but, unfamiliar with the feeling, had not been able to put a word to it. He had suspected Verlang—and Tresh wondered whether the black mage had indeed established a sensory connection to the pair. Tresh himself had detected nothing—but then, having extended himself, he was not strong enough to detect a black mage who wished to avoid discovery.

Now he began to hear other voices, closer to his ear. No, just one voice: female. His right arm jerked. Suddenly his left cheek stung as if struck by hot brine. His vision blurred, and darkness began to set in. Had Verlang found him? His mind did not feel the needles of evil, like the waking of a leg or arm that had gone to sleep. And Verlang was not female. He closed his eyes, even though they were already closed.

The name staked his heart. "*Tresh!*"

A report like a firework, and again his cheek stung.

The voice was now choked with tears. "Tresh. Oh, please come back to me, *please.*"

The name breathed its way into his mind: Atonya.

She was shaking him, none too gently.

He opened his eyes to hers, pools of sapphire glistening with tears. He knew without seeing that he was stretched out on one of the beds, his head supported by a pillow. Of its own accord, his right hand went to her cheek. His fingertips caressed her skin. The hand and its arm fell back to the comforter.

Atonya drew her legs up, nudged him aside for more room, and sat beside him on the bed. He tried to speak to her, and found himself unable to emit even a sound. The palm of her hand was cool across his forehead, but damp for he was sweating profusely. If the salty droplets put her off, it did not show in her expression. For just a moment, Tresh thought she was the loveliest creature he had ever seen. Belatedly he understood that his emotional response stemmed from relief that he had emerged from his trance in the company of someone he knew. Under the circumstances, he was as safe as he could be.

Utterly spent, Tresh allowed his eyes to close. The girl got up. Presently he felt a cold cloth across his forehead. Her voice reached him as if carried along on a spring breeze.

"You frightened me, Tresh."

A tear welled in the corner of his eye, and puddled there, waiting.

Atonya did something remarkable and unexpected then: he felt her lips, soft as flower petals, on his cheek.

His heart beat faster, and his breathing deepened. He found strength enough for a word. "Sorry."

"Can you sit up?" she asked.

Surprisingly, he found that he could. Liberated, the single tear plummeted down his cheek.

She fluffed his pillow behind him, and added her own to it, then sat down on the bed, facing him. The cloak concealed her. Not from modesty, he sensed, which in any case had flown the coop, but to avoid distraction. During the time he had been entranced, she had changed. What had she seen? Or heard?

"Atonya," he croaked.

She brought a cup to his lips, and he sipped at it.

"You were trembling, shaking," she told him. "Something greatly disturbed you. I had to try to bring you out of it. I *had* to, Tresh. I couldn't . . . couldn't let you . . ."

"It's all right. Did I say anything?"

"Fragments," she answered. "You spoke in an accent. Words I have not heard you use. 'Reckon,' and a single form of 'be.' And 'oos,' which might have been 'us.'"

"It was. Those two men come from the coast."

She frowned. "But . . . but they were wearing Nadua livery."

"Do you recall ever hunting with your father and mother?" he asked.

The question made her sit back, arms braced behind her for support. Her lips worked, as if searching for words. "I-I don't know," she said. "I-I think so."

"Did they go out dressed as royalty?"

"Oh, no, they would not want to be recognized."

The response confirmed to Tresh a dark suspicion.

"Why?" she cried. "What's wrong?"

He tried to stand, and found he was still too weak. "They may already be here, Atonya," he said. "And I think they're going to be assassinated."

Her eyes and mouth opened wide. For a moment she was speechless. "Oh, we have to stop this!" she wailed. "Tresh, do something."

The candles in the sconces flared up. The glazing in the window cracked.

Tresh reached out for her, a calming spell on his lips. She quieted.

"We don't know where they are," he pointed out. "Almost certainly they did not register under their own names."

Atonya scrambled to her feet. "We can *find* them."

The window shattered, and glass fell. Dust fell from the ceiling. Tresh's heart raced. If the action of magic should be sensed by Verlang, he would have to locate the source of it."

"Atonya," he said, as gently as possible. He set his hands on her shoulders. "A search will only serve to rush the event. The fact is . . . Atonya, they may already be . . . gone."

A spark lit the room briefly, before a black cloud billowed down from the ceiling. Tresh summoned a dispelment and hoped it was powerful enough; he dared not summon anything stronger.

The cloud hovered, poised.

Atonya glanced up. "Tresh? What's going on?"

"It is important that you calm yourself," he told her, trying not to alarm her further. "I told you, you have a dark seed. You must learn control before you summon its powers."

Her eyes widened. "Is that what I'm doing? Summoning them?"

"Not intentionally," he said, releasing her. "But they are within you."

"But my parents?"

The door fell from its hinges and onto the floor, and a slender, golden-haired man in an indigo cloak entered. "Are already dead," he said, finishing her thought. "You're the last of the bloodline."

"Verlang," said Tresh, masking his despair.

"I thought I recognized you," Verlang said easily. "You may abandon whatever thoughts of opposition you have brewing." He raised a closed fist. "I'm holding a heart rune. You know what that means."

The candles inflamed higher.

"What?" cried Atonya. "What does he mean?"

Verlang's smile seemed to chill the room. "Ah, it seems I have a protégée. But you're the defrocked tutor, Tresh. You explain."

Tresh licked his lips. "Squeezing it puts

51

pressure on my heart," he said. "The tighter he squeezes, the greater the pressure, until the heart stops, unable to beat."

"That's horrid!" Atonya wailed.

Dust rained down. The candles blew out completely. The last of the glazing shattered onto the walkway outside. A spark streaked down from the cloud, accompanied by sizzling.

Verlang regarded her with closer attention. "It seems your usefulness continues, after all," he said. "I look forward to instructing you."

"Never!" shouted Atonya.

Thunder sounded.

The pressure on Tresh's heart made him drop to one knee. His hand clawed at his chest.

"*Tresh!*" Atonya screamed.

Support studding cracked and splintered.

Verlang waved his free hand. Atonya collapsed onto the floor.

Tresh passed out.

♋   ♋   ♋

Uneven cobblestones rounded by weather and use made Tresh stagger along the path through the tavern gardens. Verlang's control spell was too strong for him to counter directly. With no need to see him or Atonya, the black mage walked some five paces ahead of them. She too appeared to be functioning under a control spell, though not as strong as the one that bound Tresh. Verland did not particularly fear her, then.

The fate Verlang intended for Atonya remained uncertain. Tresh recalled that he seemed eager to have another student. But then why had she been brought along? Or did Verlang not trust her out of his sight?

Tresh continued to wobble. Try as he might to regain his equilibrium, it failed him. He walked as if he were inebriated. Atonya, beside him, kept her eyes straight ahead as she strolled. The path led to the river, half a kilometer from the tavern. It seemed an excellent place to dispose of an unwanted body. Tresh figured his would travel far downstream before it was recovered. So too would Atonya's, if that was to be her fate.

He shifted his gaze to the distance. A quarter of a kilometer to the river; not that he could see it, but the ragged row of trees, including several willows, that grew along the near bank betrayed its location. His mind felt as unsteady as his gait. No plans for escape materialized. His hands flexed with the desire to act, to do something, anything. His travel bag, with his runes and amulets, remained back in the room—or perhaps Verlang had confiscated it. Tresh possessed a spell that would reverse the control—but his mouth refused to work; he was unable to utter it.

Verlang glanced back; his smile chilled Tresh. He *knew*! And he was confident of his superiority. Tresh had been barred from invoking a spell against him.

Tresh tried to gain Atonya's attention as they trod through a puddle left by the recent storm. A wave of his hand made her falter, confirming that Verlang's control over her was weak. She was no threat to the black mage.

"Are you all right?" he asked, surprising himself. He kept his voice low. "Atonya?"

She did not look at him. "Yes," she whispered. "What's going to happen?"

"I don't know," he lied.

"Do I deserve that?"

Tresh's face twisted with emotion and pain. "No, Atonya, of course not."

"You're just trying to protect me," she said. "Thank you, but I don't need it."

A long and fairly straight branch lay on the grass, blown there from a tree during the storm. Tresh reached down for it, more to see whether he could rather than actually to pick it up. Unexpectedly, his hand and body functioned. So there were limits to the control spell, he thought, as he plucked the side branches off to fashion a walking stick.

"He's going to kill me," said Tresh. "He'll toss my body into the river. Or have it tossed," he added, with a glance over his shoulder at the two men in livery, following several paces behind.

"I can't step off the path," she said.

"I know. You're under a spell. So am I."

"What can we do?"

A possibility flashed through his mind, and he shunted it aside lest Verlang detect a rise in hope.

"By myself, nothing directly," he answered. "Nor can you, I daresay. But together we might accomplish something. Control your emotions, Atonya. Allow yourself no feelings at all."

"You ask much of me."

His voice felt hollow. "My life depends on it."

"You know I will help you," she said softly. "What is it that I must do?"

They splashed through another puddle, unable to step around it.

"Could you be angry, enraged?" he asked.

"Easily."

"When the time comes, I want you to build it up suddenly, in a burst of fury, with your eyes and focus, your whole being, on Verlang. Until then, remain as calm and steady as possible."

"What are you going to do?" she wanted to know.

He hefted the make-shift walking stick. "Distract him."

She dropped her voice to a low whisper. "What about the two behind us?"

"If this works, and if needs be, I shall deal with them." He surveyed the path ahead. "We're about to step through another puddle. I'll act just after we cross it. Are you—?"

"Oh, I'm ready," she growled darkly.

Tresh was less certain regarding his own preparedness. Verlang's spell protected himself from a direct counter from Tresh. But did that include Atonya? More importantly, did it include all arcane actions?

Tresh drew a deep breath and let it out slowly, steadying himself insofar as that was possible. He continued to walk as if both legs ached.

"Tresh?" said Atonya.

"Not yet."

"Are you sure this will work?"

"No."

"But it's our only chance," she said dully. "I get that. Tresh?"

He felt her hand on his arm, and turned his face to hers.

"It will work," she declared.

As they approached the puddle, Tresh saw on the other side of it what he had hoped to find. Ahead of them, Verlang was walking as if he hadn't a care in the world. Tresh was unable to determine whether that attitude affected the strength of the control spell, but it scarcely mattered, because he had no intention of directly attacking the black mage.

Water splashed from under Tresh's feet. He used the walking stick like a cane, to aid him with each step he took, until finally he and Atonya reached the other side of the puddle. There, he lifted the stick and, uttering a brief malediction, drove it down as hard as he could, directly onto a wet footprint left by Verlang. The black mage cried out in pain and stumbled, grasping his wounded foot.

"Now!" shouted Tresh.

Atonya's voice was raw, and charged with hatred. Her face darkened and twisted. "I'll kill you, you bastard!" she shrieked. "You killed my parents, I'll kill you."

Verlang burst into flames, and exploded. So did a shrub behind him. A line of fire ran across the grass all the way to the treeline.

Liberated, Tresh spun around, preparing to hurl an incantation. The two men in livery, their mouths agape, turned and fled.

Sobbing, Atonya collapsed onto the wet grass.

Tresh dropped to a knee beside her, and put his arms around her shoulders, pulling her to him. He who knew many complex and strange words to say now struggled to find simple ones. He did not know whether she wept for her parents, or for her release from Verlang, or whether it was relief from the fear she had just undergone. In the end, he thought, it did not matter. This was a bird fallen from a nest; she needed but to fly.

He nuzzled his lips against her hair, and kissed her. She sniffled, and pulled away, and locked her eyes on his.

"Are you going to make a habit of this?" she asked

Tresh just looked at her, confused.

"Every time I get tossed away, you're there to pick me up," she explained.

He smiled, and abruptly withdrew from her.

Erin, he thought, and *I can't, not again.* It was enough to have rescued this girl, now no longer a girl but a queen in her own right. Sadness beset him.

They got to their feet.

"We have to find her," she told him.

He did not have to ask who she meant. Unsteadily at first, they walked back toward the tavern, gaining strength as they went. Once inside, a simple inquiry gave them the room number. It turned out to be located just down the hall from their own.

Atonya rapped on the door. Her knuckles hurt, and she shook her hand. A tear-choked voice bade them enter, and they complied.

The girl was sitting on the bed, shoulders hunched, eyes still streaming with tears. She looked at them without really seeing them at first. Then Atonya came into focus, and she shot to her feet.

"You're me!" she cried. "How can that be?"

Atonya said, "I am she whom you were going to replace." She stated her name without honorific.

"But that is my name," said the girl. Frowning, she shook her head. "No, that is the name he told me to call myself."

Tresh started to ask the obvious question. A slash of Atonya's hand stopped him.

"And what is your real name?" asked Atonya.

"Mearad Fuller. I am . . . my father works with tapestries. Then you must be . . ." She dropped to her knees on the floor, and hung her head.

"Rise, Lady Mearad," said Atonya.

Mearad remained as she was. "I am no Lady, Milady."

"You are now. I shall require a Lady-in-

Waiting. Rise, please."

The girl stood up—straighter, thought Tresh, and with a bit of pride.

"Verlang is dead," Atonya informed her. "You are safe."

Tresh kept his counsel. Breeding, he thought, will always out. Atonya had become herself. He cast about for her aura, and found it bright orange —she would bring order to chaos.

"He killed my . . . your parents," said Mearad.

"Where are they?" Atonya asked gently.

"In . . . in the next room. He was going to announce a tragic hunting accident, and I was to be invested." Again she hung her head. "I am sorry, Milady."

"Where is the castellan?" asked Atonya.

"In Nadua, Milady."

Still Tresh did not speak. It pleased him to watch Atonya grow, knowing that he'd had something to do with that. If her development was atonement for his past, so much the better. He could go on, now.

Atonya turned to him. "Please make arrangements for our immediate departure," she instructed. "There is a royal carriage by the stable. Quietly have my parents placed inside it, under cover. And find the coachman; have him assist." For a moment she faltered. "I-I . . . do not know what else to do, Tresh. Whatever needs to be done, please do it for me."

He bowed. "Of course, Milady."

♋   ♋   ♋

In the royal carriage, Atonya said little, and Mearad waited patiently for instructions that never came, while Tresh was lost in his own thoughts. Originally he had set out for Nadua to seek employment as a tutor. Waylaid by altruism, he'd had no choice other than to see to the girl on the dump. It seemed so long ago, even if it was only early this morning. So much had happened, in one day. Even now, as darkness enveloped them, he felt as if there were more to come. What it might be, he had no idea.

As they reached the gates of Nadua, Atonya said, "You're awfully quiet."

A weak smile crossed his mouth. "I'm just weary."

"As am I. But I cannot afford to be weary.

"You are, or are about to be, the Princess of Nadua," Tresh pointed out. "You can feel whatever emotion strikes you. There are some emotions, however, that you should conceal from your people."

"Still teaching me, are you?"

"I didn't mean—"

"Certainly you did." She touched his arm. "And thank you."

"Is that 'I thank you' or 'We thank you?'"

She turned on the seat and fixed him with sapphire eyes. "I have known you for but one day," she said quietly. "And I will never use a 'royal we' with you."

Tresh looked away; he had to. They rode the rest of the way in silence.

Arrived at the castle, Tresh was assigned to a room on the second level, normally reserved for immediate family and relatives. At first he was reluctant to accept it, but he was loathe to hurt Atonya. The room's furnishings reminded him of those he'd known in Eridania, which in turn reminded him of Erin and of his transgression. The result was a fitful slumber in which the dreams faded from memory as he awoke from them. He thought that was merciful of them.

He washed and dressed—someone, probably a chambermaid acting on Atonya's instructions, had laid out clothing for him. He also found some rolls and butter and cheese and thin slices of meat, all on a silver serving tray; and some fresh water in a silver ewer. He thought it unusual that he had not awakened during their delivery.

For perhaps an hour after he had eaten, he sat around wondering what he ought to do next. Surely Atonya was busy with preparations for the coronation, which had to be held as soon as possible for continuity's sake. From the development he had witnessed of her in just one day, he knew she would do well as Princess. She had the gifts of compassion, and of place—she had treated her double with the simple respect due any other human being. He would not worry about her after he departed.

And he had to leave. They had shared a day, but there had been unspoken moments, at least for him. A moment of weakness—no, he could not, dared not, countenance that.

His mind firmed now, he rose, and slipped on his travel bag and water skin, and stepped from the room into a hallway that he did not quite recall. Sounds of activity reached his ears, but from below. Voices entered through the window at the far end of the hallway. A crowd had gathered outside, presumably to witness the investiture. Beside the window was a door that led out onto a balcony.

Moved by curiosity, he had taken but a few steps toward the window, when Atonya emerged from her room. Already she was attired in a regal strapless gown whose shade of blue matched her eyes. Fabric swished even with her gentle steps, by feet barely visible under the long skirt, clad in soft blue velvet. Her eyes saddened when she saw that he was packed for traveling.

She drew up before him, and spread her hands like a mendicant. "Why?" she asked.

"I think you know very well why, Milad—"

"Don't . . . don't you dare!" she whispered, hissing. "I am Atonya," she insisted. "You are Tresh."

Pain slugged him. He shut his eyes against it. "That only makes it worse." Her touch on his arm opened his eyes again. "Stay," she pleaded.

"You don't know what you—"

Her eyes widened, and began to glisten. "But I *do*," she said earnestly. "I *do* know what I am asking."

Tresh looked away. His face twisted. "I-I . . . I'm sorry." He looked at her once more, memorizing her face, her lines. "I wish you well, Mi-Princess Atonya."

He found the strength to turn and walk away.

The steps grew easier. He had taken perhaps ten of them when he heard her call, softly, "I-I'm going to need a vizier."

He slowed, and stopped, and stood very still for a long moment.

And turned back around.

Sarrow
By Tyree Campbell

The oceans have evaporated as the Earth warmed. It is a time of desolation as the remnants of humanity live in small settlements scattered on what once was the ocean floor. Men are paramount, women are breeders. People do what they can to get by.

One breeder dares to say "No!" to all this: Sarrow. Refusing to breed, and more skilled and resourceful than most men, she sets off to seek her identity and her destiny. Along the way she encounters Karthan, a kindred spirit. Like her, he searches for himself. They are equals.

But the elements conspire against them: earthquakes, salt storms, volcanos, flash floods. And there are raiding parties who seek to capture and sell slaves. Where are Sarrow and Karthan to go?

Up, says Sarrow. I believe in you, says Karthan. Thus the perilous journey back to the land begins.

https://www.hiraethsffh.com/product-page/sarrow-by-tyree-campbell

The Butterfly and the Sea Dragon

A Yoelin Thibbony Rescue

By Tyree Campbell

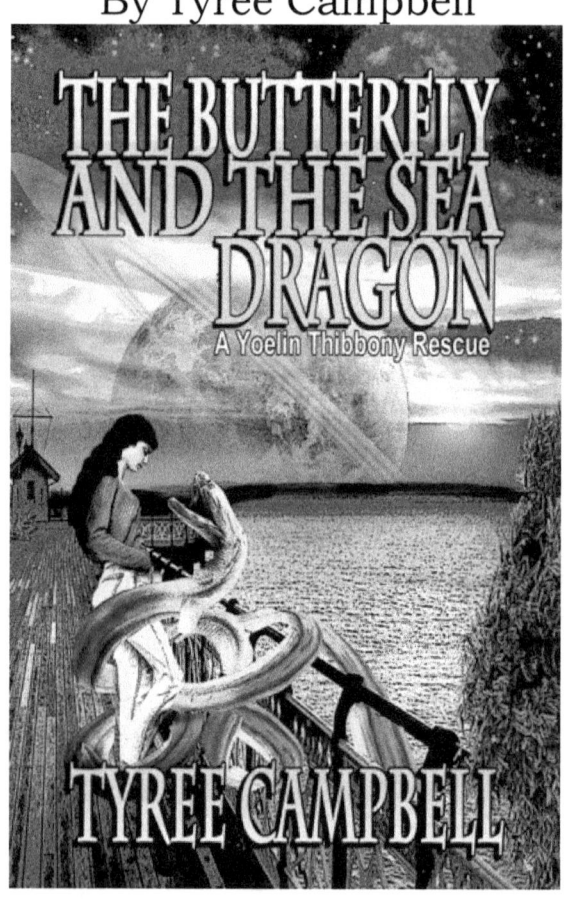

Here's how it starts:
"The only records that delineate and authenticate Corporatia territories are on that Palmetto. We want it back."

"What happened?" Yoelin asked.

"A records clerk bypassed security, recorded the information and then deleted it from our computers, and departed for Havelox Rest, outside our jurisdiction, where we believe she is now."

After the words "Havelox Rest," Yoelin heard only the pounding of her heart. A wave of dizziness passed. *Why there? Why did it have to be* there?

So who's Yoelin Thibbony? That's what she calls herself now. She endured a cruel and abusive childhood, when there was no one to rescue her. Now she performs Rescues of people or things—sometimes for hire, sometimes for free. She's been hired to retrieve stolen archives. But to perform this Rescue, Yoelin has to return to Havelox Rest, the world of her childhood—a world that still holds dark and bleak terrors for her.

https://www.hiraethsffh.com/product-page/the-butterfly-and-the-sea-dragon-by-tyree-campbell

www.ingramcontent.com/pod-product-compliance
Lightning Source LLC
LaVergne TN
LVHW012037060526
838201LV00061B/4643